This is Chummy.

This is Chummy's gran.

Chummy and his gran ADORE each other!

Carrots are money in Bunnyland.

For komachi, my wee bundle
of love and gratitude

LADYBIRD BOOKS

UK | USA | Canada | Ireland | Australia
India | New Zealand | South Africa

Ladybird Books is part of the Penguin Random House group of companies
whose addresses can be found at global.penguinrandomhouse.com.

www.penguin.co.uk   www.puffin.co.uk   www.ladybird.co.uk

Penguin
Random House
UK

First published 2020 by Nancy Paulsen Books,
an imprint of Penguin Random House LLC, New York, USA
This edition published in Great Britain by Ladybird Books Ltd 2022
001

Original design by Marikka Tamura
Text hand-lettered by Cinders McLeod

Printed in China

The authorized representative in the EEA is Penguin Random House Ireland,
Morrison Chambers, 32 Nassau Street, Dublin D02 YH68

A CIP catalogue record for this book is available from the British Library

ISBN: 978-0-241-52750-4

All correspondence to:
Ladybird Books, Penguin Random House Children's
One Embassy Gardens, 8 Viaduct Gardens
London SW11 7BW

On Chummy's birthday, his gran gave him
10 carrots...

Spend some on yourself, dear,
and some on helping others.

Chummy knows
how he wants
to spend
his carrots.

He has a **MEGA** plan...

I want to

SAVE the WORLD!

The world's
a big place,
Chummy.

Okay,
then I'll
just save

BUNNYLAND!

Wait till you see me

FIGHT those DRAGONS!

So let's think about who needs to be rescued. I've heard bumblebees could use some help.

Oh, I
LOVE
bumblebees.
How can I help them?

buzzzZZZZ

Bees get their food from flowers, and we don't have enough blooming in Bunnyland any more.

I'll plant some! But what about my COSTUME?

Maybe you could start
by buying the cape.
Sometimes the best plans
start small and grow...

Just
like
me!

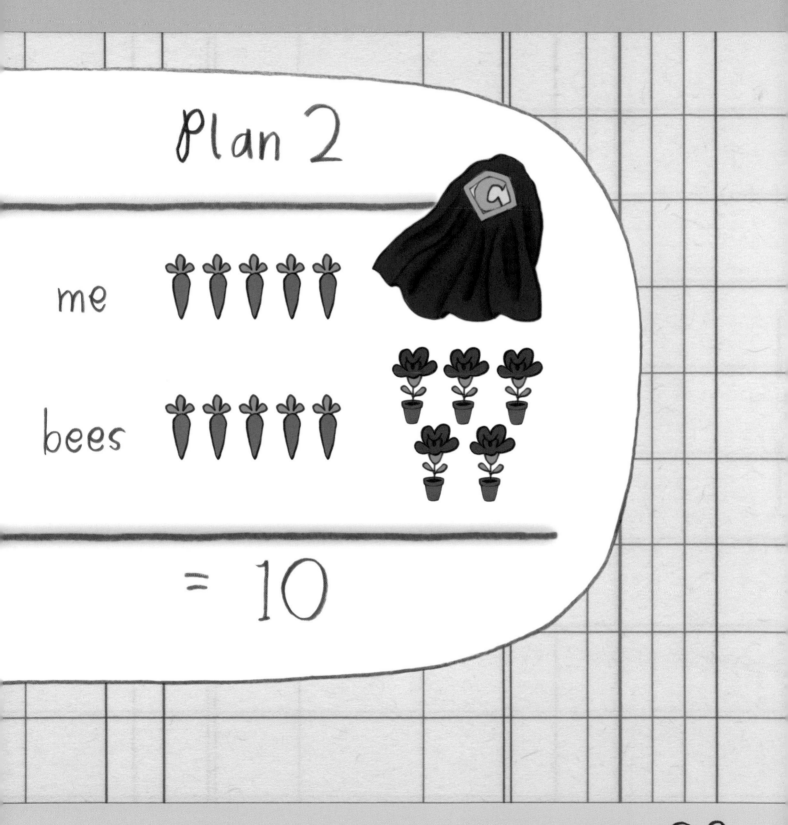

I want to help the bees. Maybe Plan 2?

It's lunchtime,
Chummy!

Yay,
I'm
SUPER
hungry!

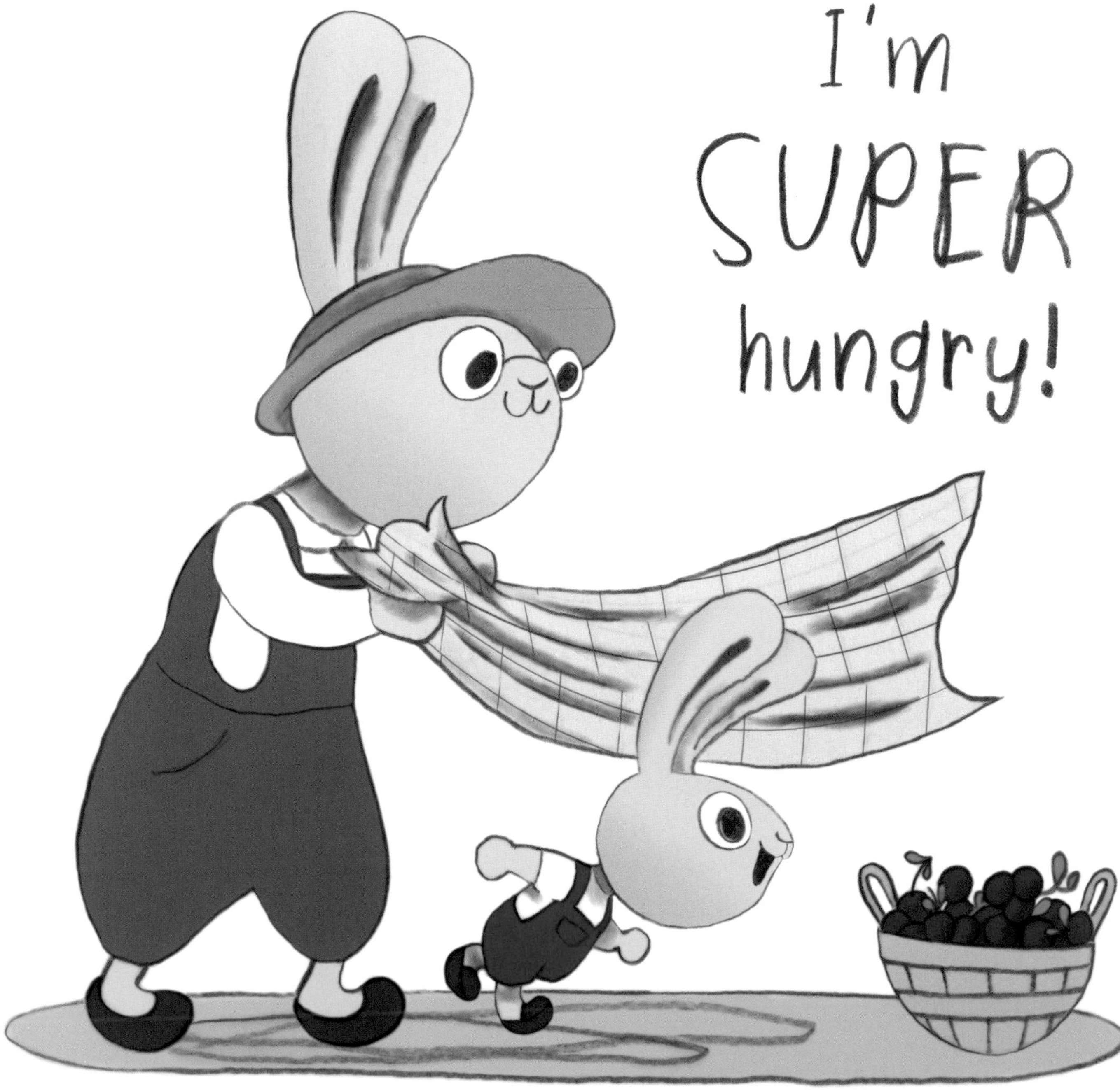

Then you know
how the bees
must feel?

I do!
Hey, I think I'll give
all
your gift
to help!

So no superhero
costume?

Maybe I don't need a costume to be a hero.

Plan 3

me ○

bees 🥕🥕🥕🥕🥕
🥕🥕🥕🥕🥕   🌹🌹
🌹🌹

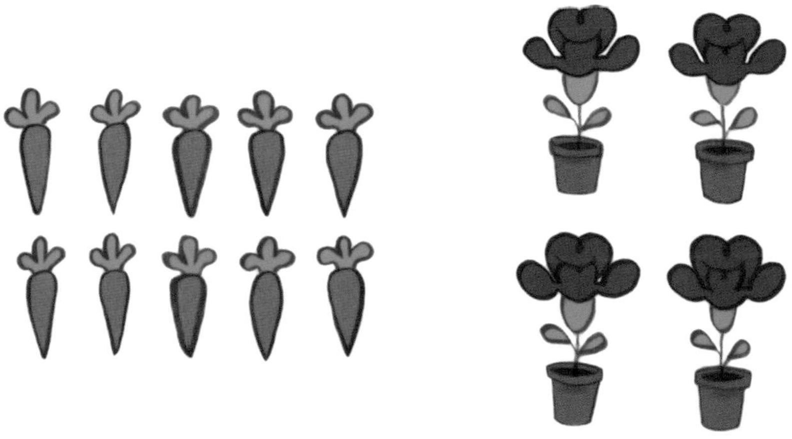

= 10

Chummy, you are quite the superbunny!

It's Chummy,
his shovel and
his snapdragons
to the rescue!

buzz

buzz... buzzzzzz

I gave and helped

It's never too early to teach your little bunny about money!

Collect all the books in the Moneybunny series:

ISBN: 978-0-241-52749-8

ISBN: 978-0-241-52752-8

ISBN: 978-0-241-52751-1

ISBN: 978-0-241-52750-4